The Lost Sunglasses

Written by
Lara Paparo

Illustrated by
Diana Nemesu

OWL PUBLISHING

One day, Blake and his mom went to the beach.

They played in the ocean and jumped in the waves…

one, two, THREE!

A big wave **CRASHED** near them and mommy's sunglasses fell off in the ocean.

3

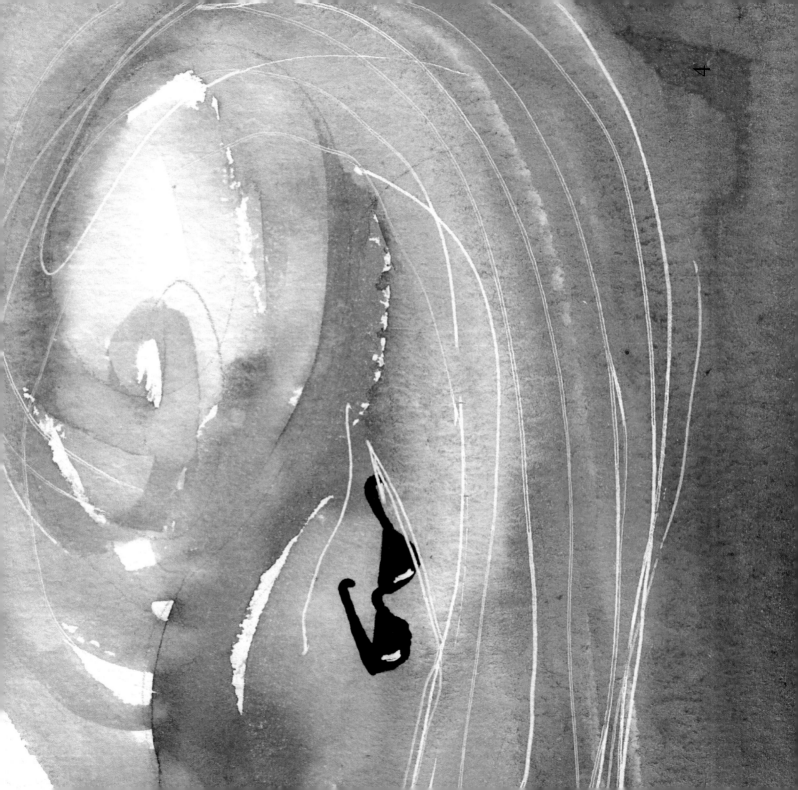

Blake was worried.

What happened to mommy's glasses?

They looked and looked in the ocean, but the glasses were not there.

"Where did they go?" Blake wondered. He was sad that the glasses were nowhere to be found.

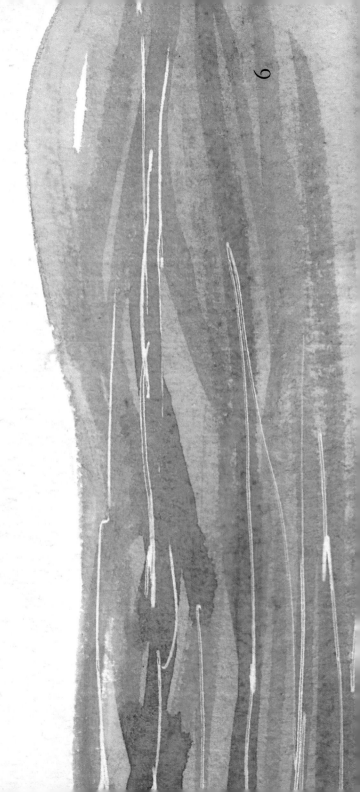

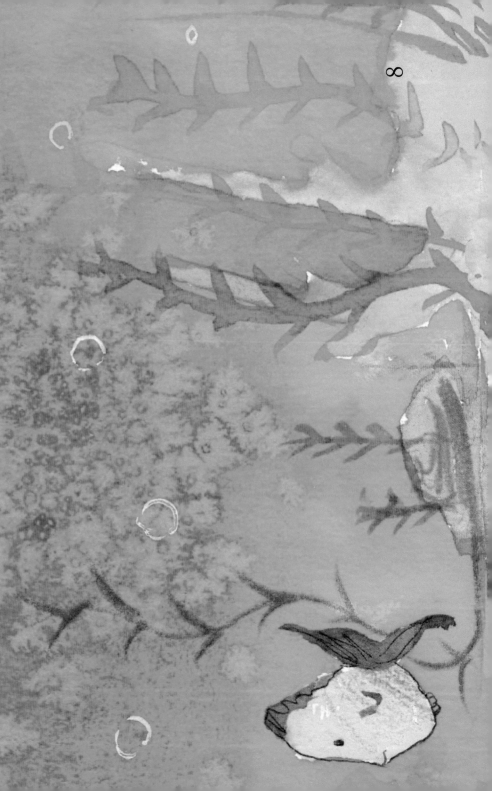

The glasses tumbled out into the ocean where a bottle nose dolphin found them.

"This is a funny thing," thought the dolphin.

She swam around with the sunglasses until a big current came and tumbled them away. The dolphin looked around, but the glasses were gone!

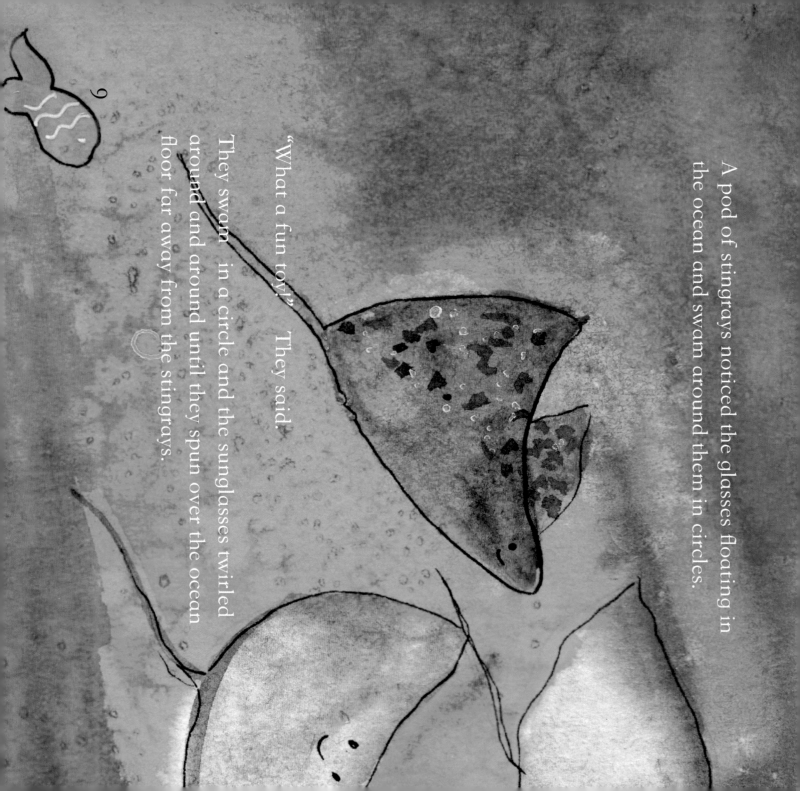

A pod of stingrays noticed the glasses floating in the ocean and swam around them in circles.

"What a fun toy!" They said.

They swam in a circle and the sunglasses twirled around and around until they spun over the ocean floor far away from the stingrays.

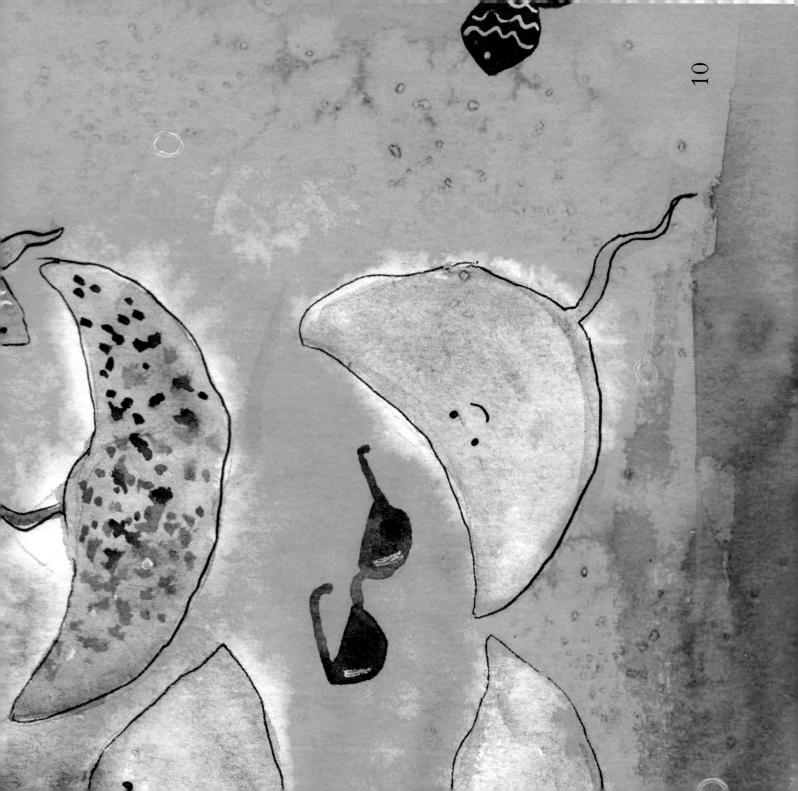

11

The glasses drifted over to a horseshoe crab who was scuttling on the floor of the ocean.

"What is this?" thought the horseshoe crab. He inspected the glasses and saw his reflection the lenses.

But then a strong current took the sunglasses far away and the horseshoe crab couldn't see himself anymore.

13

A cluster of sand crabs were scurrying across the ocean floor.

"Look at this treasure," they said, "let's take it with us!"

The sand crabs each grabbed the sunglasses and carried the new treasure away on their backs. Suddenly a Mako shark sped by and the glasses were knocked off and tumbled far away.

The glasses followed in the wake of the mako shark and flew up to his fin, where he saw the glasses.

The shark thought the glasses were a shiny fish, and he tried to take a bite out of them.

"Yuck," said the shark, "this is NOT a fish!"

The shark spit the glasses out and they shot across the ocean floor far away from the shark.

A turtle was swimming near an inlet and the glasses floated toward her. She put them on, and swam around.

"These are beautiful!" She said.

The turtle did some somersaults and the glasses fell off and drifted away from the turtle.

17

A scuba diver found the glasses as he was picking clams and mussels near the pier.

"I wonder who lost these sunglasses," he said.

He swam to the surface of the water to put the sunglasses in his boat. Suddenly, a huge seagull swooped down and took them out of his hand.

"Hey," the scuba diver yelled, but the seagull was already far away.

19

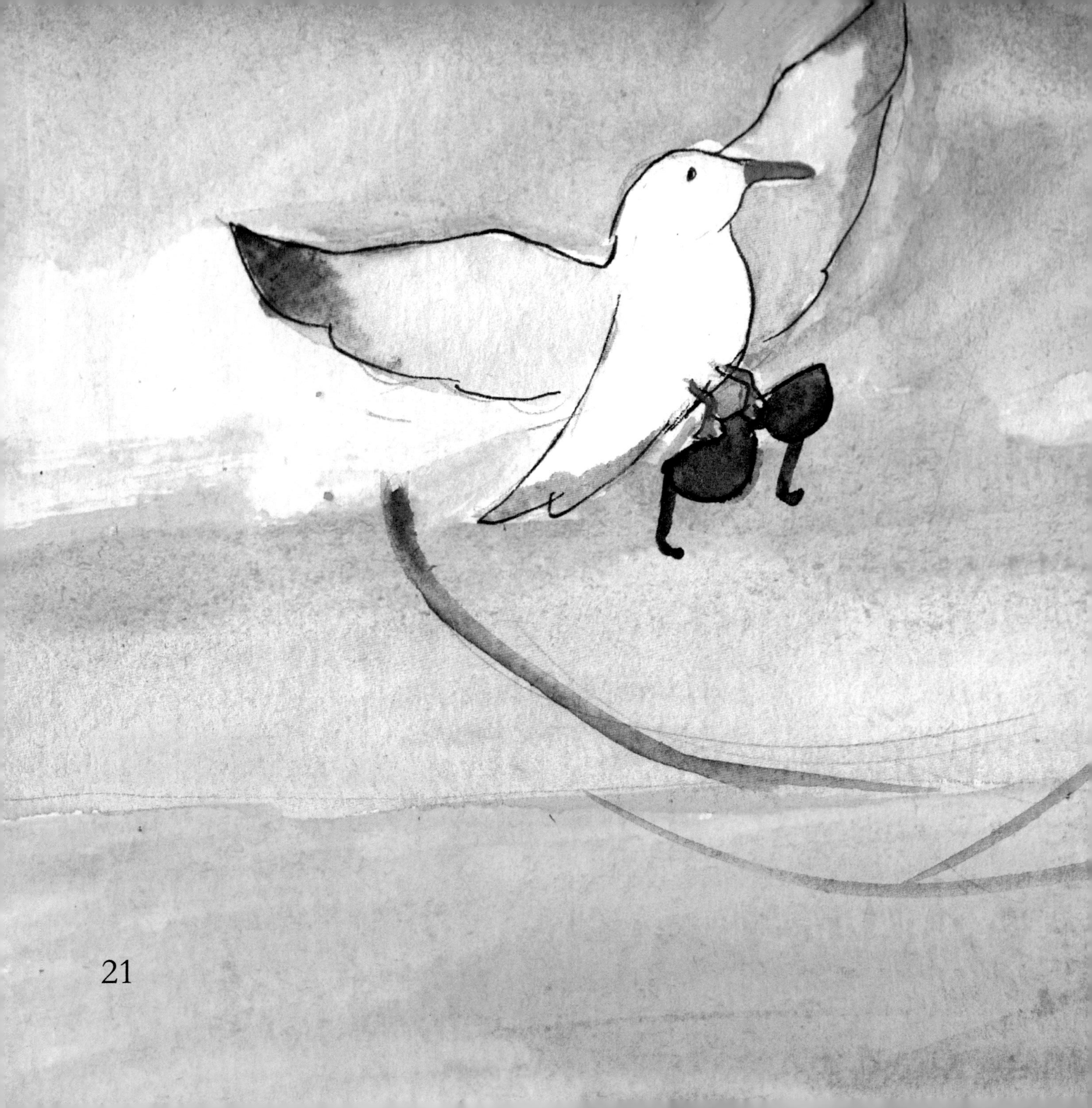

The seagull flew up and down the beach carrying the sunglasses in his feet.

He saw a little boy eating a sandwich and flew down to try and take a bite. It was Blake!

Blake saw the seagull coming and moved his sandwich away.

The seagull tried to grab the sandwich, but couldn't hold onto the sunglasses and they flew out of his feet and onto the towel next to Blake.

VENTNOR CITY

"Mommy, look!" yelled Blake.

"The seagull dropped your sunglasses onto my towel!"

"Wow!" said Blake's mommy. "This was a very lucky day."

"And these are VERY lucky sunglasses," said Blake.

For Blake and Gianna

Copyright © 2019 by Lara Paparo

ISBN: 978-1-949929-10-2

Library of Congress Control Number: In Progress

All Rights Reserved. Published by Owl Publishing, LLC.
150 Parkview Heights Road
Ephrata, PA 17522
www.owlpublishinghouse.com

OWL PUBLISHING

Made in United States
Orlando, FL
03 May 2023

32737606R00018